GHOSTBUSTERS II

COLUMBIA PICTURES PRESENTS

AN IVAN REITMAN FILM

BILL MURRAY DAN AYKROYD SIGOURNEY WEAVER
HAROLD RAMIS RICK MORANIS
"GHOSTBUSTERS II"
ERNIE HUDSON ANNIE POTTS MUSIC BY RANDY EDELMAN
EXECUTIVE PRODUCERS BERNIE BRILLSTEIN JOE MEDJUCK MICHAEL C. GROSS
WRITTEN BY HAROLD RAMIS AND DAN AYKROYD
PRODUCED AND DIRECTED BY IVAN REITMAN   A COLUMBIA PICTURES RELEASE

Ghostbusters II

A NOVEL BY
B. B. Hiller
BASED ON A MOTION PICTURE BY
Harold Ramis AND Dan Aykroyd

BASED ON THE CHARACTERS CREATED BY
Dan Aykroyd AND Harold Ramis

An Ivan Reitman Film
STARRING
Bill Murray, Dan Aykroyd, Sigourney Weaver, Harold Ramis, Rick Moranis

A YEARLING BOOK

Published by
Dell Publishing
a division of
Bantam Doubleday Dell Publishing Group, Inc.
666 Fifth Avenue
New York, New York 10103

The trademark Yearling® is registered in the U.S. Patent and Trademark Office.

ISBN: 0-440-40237-9

Printed in the United States of America

July 1989

10   9   8   7   6   5   4   3   2

CW

*This book is dedicated
to the ghost
who won't be busted.*

"Suck in the guts guys, we're the Ghostbusters."

1

$\mathcal{D}$ana Barrett was having a hard time. She held two bags of groceries with one hand and was pushing her son's baby carriage with the other. Oscar, the baby, was being fussy. People who passed her on the street stared at her because her baby was crying. Nobody offered to help her.

One grocery bag slipped out of her hand and landed on the sidewalk. Her eggs were smashed. Her marshmallows got covered with muddy slush. An apple rolled into the gutter. Before she could finish picking up the mess, she felt a rumbling beneath her—like a subway. But there was no subway under this sidewalk.

Oscar's carriage began to shake. At first it was just a little wobble, then it became more violent. Suddenly the carriage lurched and started rolling away. Uphill!

Dana chased after her baby, but the carriage kept

going faster and faster. It sped past many other people, and nobody made the slightest effort to stop it. Dana couldn't believe how rude and selfish people could be when she needed help. The carriage swerved along the sidewalk, dodging walkers, dogs, and other baby carriages. It practically flew into the middle of the street, and there it stopped as suddenly as it had begun—right in the path of a big bus!

The driver spotted the carriage in the intersection. First he slammed on the brakes, then he turned the bus as fast as he could to the right. It smashed into two parked cars. The passengers in the bus were tossed around like clothes in a dryer. But Oscar's carriage was untouched.

Dana ran out into the street and tried to push the carriage to safety. She didn't know why, but the carriage wouldn't budge. The cars, trucks, and buses that surrounded her honked loudly. She picked up her baby and fled, carrying him to the safety of the sidewalk.

As the traffic began to move again around Oscar's abandoned baby carriage, Dana watched and thought.

The last time she'd seen anything this weird was when she'd met the Ghostbusters. That had been a couple of years ago. They'd saved her life then, but it seemed like it was a different life. Since that time she'd stopped having dates with one of the Ghostbusters, Peter Venkman; she'd married somebody else; she'd had a baby. She'd even gotten a divorce. A lot had changed since then, but it seemed to Dana that some things had not.

There was something weird in her neighborhood. Dana didn't know what it was, but she knew who she had to call!

2

While Dana was struggling with Oscar and the very strange behavior of his baby carriage, some of her old friends, the Ghostbusters, were having their struggles too.

Ray Stantz and Winston Zeddemore had just entered an expensive brownstone on New York City's West Side. Ms. Gallt, the woman who led them through the house, had a worried expression on her face.

"How many of them are there, ma'am?" Stantz asked politely.

"Fourteen," she said. "They're in the back. I hope you can handle them. It's been like a nightmare!"

Ray and Winston adjusted their proton packs. They were ready for the worst—and they got it!

Then Ms. Gallt opened the door to the playroom.

There Ray and Winston saw fourteen seven-year-olds celebrating Sam Gallt's birthday!

"Oh, Ghostbusters! Boo!" yelled one of the kids.

"We wanted He-Man!" another said.

One of the little boys tossed a glob of ice cream into the air. "Oh, the floor's been slimed, Ms. Gallt!" he whined. "And *they* didn't do anything about it!" He pointed to Ray and Winston.

"Time for the song," Ray hissed to Winston. Winston pushed the PLAY button on his proton pack. The familiar theme music of the Ghostbusters began wailing, and when the song asked who they would call, the kids yelled, "He-Man!"

Ray and Winston looked at one another. Kids at birthday parties could be really obnoxious. Ray and Winston would have preferred tangling with a full-torso apparition!

Across town, Peter Venkman was having his own troubles. Since the Ghostbusters had been put out of business, he'd become a television talk-show host. His show was called *World of the Psychic with Dr. Peter Venkman.* Most of the time Venkman thought he was probably dealing with crazy people instead of ghosts. He would have preferred a full-torso apparition to what confronted him now.

"No, that's right," his guest, Sarah, said, leaning forward to reach the microphone. "The spacecraft actually landed right on top of my head. It was about the size of a dinner plate."

"I see," Venkman said.

"But it weighed more. In fact, a lot of things are heavy. Did I tell you about the overweight carrot that was working at the garage in my neighborhood? He absolutely refused to check my oil!" she huffed in anger.

"And I think your oil *needs* checking!" Venkman said sincerely.

His next guest was a man who said he had absolute *proof* that the world would end at the stroke of midnight on New Year's Eve. That was just a few weeks away. Venkman didn't like the idea. Neither did his audience. They booed the man.

The show couldn't be over soon enough to suit Venkman!

"Where do you find these people, Norman?" Venkman asked his producer when they were in the hallway after the show. "I thought we were having the guy who bends spoons with telekinetic power."

"A lot of the better psychics won't come on the show," Norman said. "They think you don't believe them."

"I'll tell you what I don't believe," Venkman said. "I don't believe overweight carrots! Spoon-bending can be total reality compared to overweight carrots."

Just then there was a commotion down the hall outside another studio at the television station. The mayor of the city had just finished giving an interview.

"Hey, there's Lenny! Yo! Lenny! Mr. Mayor!" Venkman yelled, chasing the mayor down the hallway. "We're old friends," he explained to Norman.

The mayor's bodyguard stepped in Venkman's way. One of the mayor's aides smiled at Venkman, but he didn't look like he meant the smile at all.

"I'm Jack Hardemeyer, the mayor's assistant," the smiling man said. "What can I do for you?"

"I just wanted to say hello to His Honor," Venkman said. "We're old friends."

"I know who you are, Dr. Venkman. Busting any ghosts lately?" he asked snidely.

"No," Venkman said. "That's what I want to talk to Lenny about. It wasn't really fair the way the city yanked our licenses after the last job we did. I thought Lenny ought to know . . ."

"I think Lenny knows everything he needs to know about Ghostbusters," Hardemeyer said. He nodded at the bodyguard, who released Venkman. The bodyguard and Hardemeyer then hurried down the hallway, following after the mayor, who was safely out of Venkman's reach by then.

Venkman tried to smooth his shirt where the bodyguard had been holding it.

"Tell Lenny that, because of you, I won't vote for him!" he yelled to Hardemeyer.

The only answer he got was the slam of an elevator door.

He longed for the days when the Ghostbusters were kings—saving the city from the ghosts that had invaded it.

He'd show them. One day he'd show the whole world again!

3

The baby carriage followed Dana home. When she got about a block from her house, it suddenly started acting completely normal—which is to say it stopped acting at all. She put Oscar in it and took him home.

As soon as she'd locked the door behind her, she called Egon Spengler. He'd been a Ghostbuster, but since the Ghostbusters had been outlawed, he was doing research. Dana thought she had something new for him to research. He sounded glad to hear from her, but he was busy and couldn't talk to her until that afternoon. They agreed to meet at his lab. That was all right with Dana; she had some work to do at the museum that morning.

She left Oscar with the baby-sitter and told the woman not to take him out of the apartment. She was pretty sure they'd be safe there, especially since she'd left the carriage out in the hallway.

Dana was working at the Manhattan Museum of Art, helping to restore paintings. She was doing that because she loved art and because she could do it part-time, working when she wanted to. That was good since Oscar was so young. She packed up her paint box and headed for the museum.

The museum was just a few blocks from Dana's apartment. It was a very big building on the edge of Central Park. Dana walked up the long, wide staircase and entered one of the many doors that led to the main hallway. She showed her pass at the desk and walked through the ancient Egyptian collection, past the pharaoh's tomb and the mummies to the restoration studio on the ground floor of the building.

As she entered it she saw her co-worker, Janosz Poha, hard at work on a portrait. Janosz had been working on this painting for a long time. Dana was glad he was doing it and not she. The painting gave her the creeps. It was a full-figure portrait of somebody called Vigo the Carpathian. Vigo was a tall man, wearing a long black cape lined with shiny red silk. He had a long face, with a small pointed beard. His eyes were beady. Sometimes Dana even thought they glowed with a wicked shine. His eyebrows made little upside-down V's over his eyes. One was arched, which made Vigo look permanently cruel. Dana shuddered. Every day that Janosz worked on the painting, Vigo looked more lifelike—and more horrible.

Dana took the cover off the painting she was working on. It was a pretty English landscape with rolling hills, blue skies, and contented cows grazing in a valley. She prepared to begin her work.

"Still working on the Turner?" Janosz asked, startling her. He always seemed to startle her. Dana didn't like him much more than she liked the painting he was working on. The difference was that the painting didn't always try to ask her out on dates! She'd thought of three hundred and fifty different ways to say no to Janosz. She had the feeling that she was about to have to come up with number three hundred and fifty-one!

"You are doing good work," Janosz told her. He spoke with an accent. Instead of *work*, it sounded like *voork* when he said it. It reminded Dana of Count Dracula. "You may be ready to assist me soon. We could do good work together."

"Thank you, Janosz," she said politely. "But now that my baby is a little older, I was thinking of rejoining the orchestra. I used to play the cello, you know. I just stopped so I wouldn't have to travel with the orchestra so much." There was number three hundred and fifty-one.

"I'll be sorry to lose you," Janosz said. "Perhaps I could take you to lunch today?"

"Actually, I'm not eating lunch today. I have an appointment." Three fifty-two. Dana looked at her watch. Although she had just gotten to the studio, she really didn't want to stay there with Janosz anymore. "In fact, I'd better go," she said, putting the cover back on her painting.

"Every day I ask you and every day you've got something else to do. Do I have bad breath or something?"

Dana shrugged. "I'm sorry. Perhaps some other time." Three fifty-three.

She gathered up her belongings and hurried out of the studio. She could feel Janosz's eyes follow her with longing. And she thought she could feel another pair of eyes too. But that wasn't possible, was it?

4

". . . and then the baby carriage just suddenly stopped dead in the middle of the street," Dana said, finishing telling her chilling tale to Egon Spengler.

"Did anyone else see this happen?" he asked, only slightly distracted by the device he was using to conduct his own experiment.

"Hundreds of people. Believe me, I didn't imagine this!"

"I'm not saying you did. I was just looking for a simple explanation." He continued fiddling with the switches and dials on the little black box in front of him. He called it a Giga-meter.

"What are you working on, Egon?" Dana asked.

"I'm trying to determine whether human emotional states have a measurable effect on the psychomagnetheric energy field. It's a theory Ray Stantz and I were working on when we had to dissolve Ghostbusters."

Dana sighed. Ghostbusters were always talking about things that were impossible to understand. *Psychomagnetheric?* "You mean you're trying to figure out if people's feelings affect their environment?"

Egon looked at her in surprise and nodded. He was impressed that she'd figured it out. "I'd like to bring Ray in on your case if that's all right with you," he said, returning to the subject of Oscar's mysterious carriage.

"Okay," she agreed. She wanted to ask him some questions, but Egon's experiment began and he had to push buttons on the little black box. He was very busy.

Dana gave him a piece of paper. "This is my address and telephone number," she said. "Will you call me?"

"Certainly," Spengler said, distractedly shoving the paper into his pocket. He had to get back to his experiment. When Dana left he barely noticed her departure.

Dana got a real surprise when the Ghostbusters showed up at her door the next day. She was expecting Spengler and Stantz. What she wasn't expecting was Venkman. She wasn't sure she was ready to see Peter Venkman again. They had gone out together for a long time, and soon after they'd broken up she'd gotten married. She thought about Peter for a minute. He could be so funny—and so infuriating!

"Hello, Peter," she said nervously.

"You know, Dana, I'm very hurt that you didn't call me first. I'm still into all this stuff, you know. Haven't you ever seen my show?"

Dana smiled to herself. It was the same old Peter!

"I have seen your show," she told him. "That's why I didn't call you first!" She loved to tease him.

While Dana and Venkman traded insults Spengler and Stantz began examining Oscar and his carriage. Spengler had his black box with him.

"You should have married me, you know," Venkman said.

"You never asked me," she reminded him.

"Well, I'm very sensitive," he told her. "I need to feel love and desire."

"If you're so sensitive, how come you started introducing me as 'the old ball and chain'?"

Venkman shrugged. "I may have a few personal problems," he admitted. "But one thing I am is a total professional."

He turned to go to work with Spengler and Stantz. He didn't see Dana try to stifle a burst of laughter. She had always found him funny—and it was still true.

Spengler was measuring Oscar carefully.

"What are you going to do, Egon? Knit him a snowsuit?" Venkman asked. Egon ignored the question. Venkman picked Oscar up and began playing with him. He pretended Oscar was attacking him. "Help! Please, somebody help me. He's gone berserk!" Oscar gurgled happily at the funny faces Venkman made.

Dana was glad Venkman was having fun playing with Oscar.

"Nothing in here," Spengler announced, looking at his black box again. "If anything was going on, it's totally subdued now. I think we should see if we can find anything abnormal on the street."

Venkman handed the baby back to Dana. "Finding

something abnormal on the street in this town is a piece of cake."

Everybody ignored that remark.

Dana led the Ghostbusters down to the street. She showed them where the carriage had started moving. Then she showed them the exact spot where it had stopped—in the middle of the intersection. There was still glass on the street from the smashed cars.

Stantz took out his P.K.E. meter. It measured psycho-kinetic energy. He flipped the switch. They waited anxiously. Nothing happened. "Not a trace," Stantz said.

"Why don't we try the Giga-meter?" Spengler suggested. "It measures G.E.V.'s—giga electron volts." He pulled out the little black box Dana had seen him use in his lab as well as in her apartment. He passed the box over the spot where the carriage stopped.

The machine started emitting beeps like crazy. "I think we hit the honey pot, boys," Stantz announced. "There's something brewing under the street."

It suddenly occurred to Dana that this might not be coincidence. She turned to Peter. "Do you think maybe I have some basic problem that makes me vulnerable to these supernatural things?"

"You mean like the time you got possessed and turned into a monster terror dog?" he asked, recalling their first meeting. "It's just coincidence," he assured her.

Nobody believed him.

5

few blocks from Dana's apartment Janosz was finishing his work for the day. Just a few more strokes on the bottom of the cloak and Vigo would be nearly complete. The painting still needed plenty of work, though. It had a lot of strange symbols in the background. Janosz would begin working on those the next day.

Janosz dipped his brush in the black paint to complete Vigo's cloak. But when the last stroke was finished the painting nearly exploded with a burst of red electrical energy. The shock of current traveled through Janosz's paintbrush and coursed through his entire body, throwing him to his knees on the floor. He gasped and stared in horror as Vigo came to life on the canvas.

"I, Vigo, the scourge of Carpathia, the sorrow of Moldavia, command you!"

"Command me, lord," Janosz said, nearly in a trance. He felt totally controlled by this monstrous creature he'd restored himself.

"On a mountain of skulls in a castle of pain, I sat on a throne of blood. What was will be, what is will be no more. Now is the season of evil. Find me a child that I might live again!"

Vigo lifted his arms dramatically and triumphantly. He had a sort of scepter in one hand. With it he began touching the strange symbols in the background of the painting. As he touched each one it glowed a deep electrical red and then was restored in a bright gold color. It was much faster than the work Janosz had been doing!

"Find me a child, fool!" Vigo commanded once more.

Janosz had the uncomfortable feeling that Vigo's bite was worse than his bark.

A baby . . . where could he find a baby?

6

It wasn't easy to be inconspicuous using a jackhammer. The loud noise reverberated through the streets in the area and echoed off the tall buildings. People flung open their windows and yelled. The Ghostbusters ignored them.

"I love this," Venkman told Stantz. "We're onto something really big! We'll make some headlines with this one!"

"You're nuts!" Stantz told him. "If anybody finds out about this, we'll be in serious trouble. The judge couldn't have been clearer—'No Ghostbusting'!"

"Relax. We're going to keep this whole thing nice and quiet."

He had to yell to be heard over the jackhammer.

Spengler was struggling with the jackhammer. He hadn't had an easy time. First the police had come snooping around. Venkman told them they were from the electric company. Then the electric company had come snooping around. Venkman told them they were from the telephone company. Spengler wondered when the telephone company would show up. Venkman wouldn't let him stop, though. Venkman was convinced they'd find an answer to Dana's problem if they dug deep enough.

Suddenly he hit pay dirt. There was a loud *clunk!* as the jackhammer struck metal. Quickly he and Venkman began removing the chunks of asphalt. Stantz held a flashlight over them. When the rubble was cleared they could all see it clearly. It was an old and ornate manhole cover. It had a strange logo and the letters NYPRR etched into it.

"Help me lift this manhole cover," Egon said. Together the Ghostbusters lifted the heavy thing off. What they saw then was darkness. A lot of it.

Stantz dropped a small rock into the hole. They listened to hear it hit bottom. There was a long silence.

"Wow! It's an old air shaft! It goes on forever!"

Spengler held his Giga-meter over the hole. The beeps were louder than ever. "We need a deeper reading. Somebody has to go down there," he said. Spengler and Venkman both looked at Stantz.

Stantz was elected. They snapped him into a harness and lowered him carefully into the hole, using a winch and some strong cable.

Stantz looked around him, playing the bright beam of his flashlight into the blackness that enveloped him. At first he couldn't see anything. Then, as his eyes became accustomed to the dark, he could make out something that was familiar—yet wasn't.

He had gotten through the shaft and was in a very

large open area. It looked a lot like a subway station. There was a space for tracks and a platform. The walls were tiled and had mosaics on them. They made a picture and letters. It was a little hard to read because the tiles were so shiny. He aimed the flashlight carefully and squinted. He saw NYPRR and then VAN HORNE STATION. It sounded familiar, but what was it? Then he remembered. It was the old New York Pneumatic Rail Road. It was a short line that had been in use before the subways were built. This was a piece of the city's past—but what did it have to do with the city's future?

He checked the Giga-meter. The readings were off the dial. He looked back at the wall. It was still shiny, but it was almost like it was shimmering. He looked more closely. It was shimmering, but it wasn't shiny. It was slimy, and the slime was moving!

Stantz looked below him. The tracks were covered with slime. It was deep too! Four or five feet, and rising!

"Hey, get me out of here!" he yelled on his walkie-talkie.

"What's up?" Spengler asked. Stantz told him. Spengler and Venkman wasted no time in beginning to crank the winch.

"The stuff is trying to grab me!" Stantz yowled. Spengler and Venkman cranked harder.

A car stopped by the Ghostbusters' truck. "What's the story here?" a man from the phone company demanded.

Venkman started telling the man a story when they all heard Stantz yell. "Help! Pull me up! It's alive! It's eating my boots!"

The phone company supervisor put his hands on his hips. He knew a lie when he heard it. "You ain't with the phone company or the electric company. We checked. Tell me another one."

"Gas leak?" Venkman tried, but he knew they'd lost.

Stantz yowled once more. Everybody peered into the hole. They saw Stantz struggle to get as high as he could. Venkman and Spengler began cranking the winch once more. Stantz flailed to save himself, and that worked all right except that he hit a big loose pipe underground. It broke away and careened down into the tunnel below, hitting a main electrical transmission line on the way down.

When the shower of sparks died down, so did all of the other lights in the entire neighborhood. There was a blackout, and the Ghostbusters were in deep slime with the law.

7

$\mathbb{T}$he judge glared at the Ghostbusters. "I want to make one thing very clear. The law does not recognize the existence of ghosts and I don't either. Save that malarkey for bedtime stories, okay?"

The Ghostbusters nodded. They looked to their lawyer for comfort and assurance. Louis Tully flipped desperately through a mountain of legal books. "I think you're making a big mistake here, fellows. I do mostly tax law and some probate stuff. I got my law degree at night school."

"That's all right," Spengler said, looking on the bright side. "We got arrested at night."

Jack Hardemeyer, the mayor's aide who had tangled with Venkman at the television studio, leaned over the wooden rail in the gallery to tangle with Venkman again.

"Nice going, Venkman," he said with a sneer in his

voice. "Violating the 'No Ghostbusting' order, destruction of public property, fraud, malicious mischief. Smooth move. See you in a couple of decades—at your first parole hearing." He laughed before he left the courtroom. Venkman stuck his tongue out at him.

The trial didn't go well. The police had found very incriminating evidence on the Ghostbusters' truck at the scene of the crime. They'd even found a specimen of the slime that Stantz had collected in the abandoned Van Horne Station. Hardemeyer hadn't been kidding about jail terms. Everything made them look bad—even their lawyer.

After hours of testimony, it was time for a summation. Louis knew that he hadn't produced any evidence that said anything but GUILTY. It was time to pull out all the stops.

"Your Honor," he began. "I don't think it's fair to call my clients frauds. Okay, so the blackout was a big problem for everybody. I was stuck in an elevator for about three hours and I had to go to the—oops, I guess I shouldn't say that. Anyway, I don't blame these guys because once I turned into a dog and they helped me. Thank you."

The Ghostbusters couldn't believe it. Neither could the judge. He was really angry.

"That was unquestionably the worst presentation of a case I've ever heard in a court of law! Mr. Tully, I ought to cite you for contempt. As for your clients, I find them guilty on all counts. I order you to pay fines of $25,000 each and I sentence you to . . ."

The Ghostbusters didn't hear the rest of what the judge said. They were too busy watching the jar of slime on the exhibit table. They could see that the angrier the

judge got, the angrier the slime got and the judge got *very* angry!

"Uh-oh, she's twitching," Stantz said. The slime was wiggling and waving just the way it had in the Van Horne Station. It was also growing and changing color. Just before it burst out of the jar the Ghostbusters hit the deck, hiding under the defense table.

The slime rumbled and pulsed, sending tremors through the courtroom. It almost felt like an earthquake. Suddenly two full-torso apparitions broke loose from the slime.

"Oh, no!" the judge yelled, recognizing the faces on the ghosts. "The Scoleri brothers! I tried them for murder in 1948. They were electrocuted—and now they want to kill me!"

Everybody looked at the ghosts. They certainly *looked* like they wanted to kill the judge.

"Maybe they just want to appeal," Venkman suggested.

"Stop them! Please!" The judge yelled.

The Ghostbusters were about to dash for their equipment when their lawyer did something right. He stood up and faced the judge. "Violating a judicial restraining order could expose my clients to serious criminal penalties, Your Honor. As their attorney, I'd have to advise them against it."

The Scoleri brothers were very close to the judge.

"All right!" he yowled hysterically. "I'm reversing the order. Case dismissed!"

That was it—the words they'd been waiting for. In an instant the Ghostbusters slipped into their proton packs and armed themselves with traps.

"Okay, let's heat 'em up!" Stantz said. "Set for full neutronas on stream!"

They all adjusted their settings and prepared for battle.

"Spengs, take the door," Venkman said. "Ray, let's try to work them down and into the corner!"

Spengler cut off the ghosts' only exit while Venkman and Stantz began spraying the apparitions and forcing them into a corner.

It was an easy job compared with some they'd had in the past. A few concentrated proton streams tamed down the lightning bolts the Scoleri brothers threw at them. Then all they had to do was corner them and in a few minutes the Scoleris were trapped—for good.

"Occupado!" Venkman announced, displaying the blinking ghost trap to the courtroom.

The judge, the prosecutor, and Louis all emerged from under the tables where they had hidden. The audience in the courtroom burst into applause. Photographers started snapping their pictures.

Venkman tucked the full trap into the pocket of his proton pack.

"Case closed, boys," he announced. "And Ghostbusters is back open for business!"

8

For the Ghostbusters, at last, life was returning to paranormal.

They were back in business, and the first thing they did was to make a television commercial promising a half-price special for "your supernatural elimination needs." There were gifts for customers, including thermal mugs—and balloons for the kids!

Everybody loved the commercial—everybody except Jack Hardemeyer, the mayor's assistant, who didn't love *any*thing about the Ghostbusters—and their phones began ringing off the hook.

They got back their old receptionist, Janine. And Louis, their former client, turned accountant, turned attorney, had some accounting work to do for them once more because the money was coming in. Winston Zeddemore was happy to join his friends in their renewed business too.

They opened up shop at the old firehouse again, and they spent their first earnings on a brand-new Ectomobile—Ecto-IA. Stantz's favorite part was the siren. But he liked the flashing lights and the fog horn too.

Their first calls were pretty routine supernatural apparitions. There was the ghost jogger in Central Park. The Ghostbusters checked his cardiopulmonary efficiency rate into a ghost trap with one zap of their proton beams. Then there was the ghost who was doing his Christmas shopping in a jewelry store but he'd left his credit cards at home. They bagged him in a fourteen-karat operation.

The prettiest operation was in the crystal store's showroom. Stantz identified the problem as a straight polarity reversal.

He told the manager, "Some kind of major P.K.E. storm must have blown through here and affected the silicon molecules in the glass." What that meant was that hundreds of thousands of dollars' worth of crystal and glass was suspended in the air in the store. "We'll have it fixed in a jiff," Stantz assured the manager.

They set up their electromagnetic devices in the four corners of the showroom. At Stantz's signal they activated. The room filled with colored beams of electromagnetic force and the reversed polarity problem was instantly corrected. The trouble was that that meant all the crystal crashed to the floor, shattering into hundreds of thousands of dollars' worth of smashed crystal. Each particle seemed to catch the light in a special way. The floor gleamed and sparkled.

"Beautiful!" Stantz said admiringly. Then he turned

to the manager. "Would you like to pay us in cash or with a check?" he asked.

The manager's answer was unprintable.

Life returned to normal for Dana. Oscar's carriage didn't take any more solo trips and she didn't see any other evidence of ghosts in her life. Still, she often felt uneasy—especially when she was at the museum with Janosz and the creepy painting he was restoring.

One day, when she was working on a Vermeer still life, carefully cleaning the geometric background, she heard a nicely familiar voice. "So this is what you do, huh?" It was Peter Venkman. He looked at the painting. "Say, you're really good, you know? Kind of old-fashioned, sure, but someone'll buy it."

"I didn't paint it, Peter. I'm just cleaning it," she told him. "It's an original Vermeer. It's worth about ten million dollars." Peter gawked. "But I'm sure you didn't come here to talk about art."

"As a matter of fact, I didn't," he said. "I stopped by to tell you that I haven't forgotten your problem and that we're still on the case."

Dana wanted to ask Peter if there had been any developments, but they were interrupted by Janosz, who looked at Peter very suspiciously. Peter looked at him the same way. Dana introduced them. Peter shook hands and then asked Janosz what he'd been working on.

Janosz took Peter and Dana over to the canvas where Vigo was now nearly complete. "It's a self-portrait of Vigo the Carpathian. He ruled most of Carpathia and Moldavia in the seventeenth century."

"Too bad for the Moldavians," Peter remarked, looking at the ugly portrait. There was something almost lifelike about the painting. Peter didn't like that at all.

"He was a powerful magician. A genius in many ways and quite a skilled painter," Janosz told Peter and Dana.

"He was also a lunatic and a genocidal madman," Dana said. "He slaughtered thousands of his subjects. I hate this painting and I've felt very uncomfortable since they brought it up from storage."

Peter nodded in understanding. "Yeah, not the kind of thing you want to hang in the rec room." Then Peter had an idea. "You know what it needs? . . . A fluffy little white kitten in the corner." He picked up a paintbrush and reached toward the canvas.

Dana hid her smile.

"We don't go around changing valuable paintings," Janosz said, slapping Peter's hand away. Janosz's face was getting red with outrage.

"Well, I'd make an exception in this case if I were you," Peter suggested.

Dana thought it was time for Peter to go. She led him to the door. "Good-bye, Peter," she said, pointing the way out.

"I'd like to stay," he said. "But I really don't have time to hang around here. I'll call you, okay?" Then he turned back to Janosz. "See you later, Johnny!" he called out.

Dana smiled to herself again. She didn't think Janosz liked being called Johnny, but she'd learned a long time ago that Peter Venkman was Peter Venkman and there was no stopping him.

She returned to her easel and her Vermeer. As she picked up her tools to begin work, though, she had the strangest feeling somebody—or something—was watching her. With glowing red eyes.

9

"Oh, good. You're here," Stantz said when Venkman returned to the firehouse from the museum. "Spengler and I have something really amazing to show you."

Venkman tossed his jacket on a chair and followed Stantz into the kitchen. "It's not that thing you do with your nostrils, is it?" he asked Spengler.

Stantz and Spengler ignored the question. Stantz opened the freezer and took out a plastic container that held a slime specimen from the Van Horne Station. He put the container in their microwave and thawed it. "We've been studying the stuff—"

"And now you're going to *eat* it?" Venkman interrupted.

"No, I'm restoring it to its normal state," he said as the microwave beeped. He took out the container and poured some of the slime into an experiment dish. "Now watch this," he said. Peter watched. Stantz leaned over the specimen and began yelling at it rudely. *"You worthless piece of slime! You ignorant, disgusting blob!"*

At the first sound of Stantz's unpleasant words, the slime began to bubble and swell. It changed colors, deepening to an angry red, and got bigger.

"You foul obnoxious muck!"

It doubled in size and bubbled over the edge of the experiment dish. Some of it dripped into the toaster.

"This is what you do with your spare time?" Venkman asked.

But Stantz was too excited to pay any attention to Venkman's jokes. "This is an incredible breakthrough, Venkman. It's a psycho-reactive substance! Whatever this is, it clearly responds to human emotional states."

"Mood slime," Venkman suggested. "We ought to bottle this stuff and sell it. Too late for Christmas this year, of course, but it'll be next year's Pet Rock!"

"Now let me show you the positive reactions," Stantz said. He nodded at Spengler, who picked up his guitar and strummed a few chords. Together, Spengler and Stantz began singing sweetly, "Cumbaya, my Lord, cumbaya! Oh, Lord, cumbaya!"

Immediately the slime reduced to its pre-insult size. It gurgled and bubbled sweetly, like a baby.

"Does it have any favorites?" Venkman asked.

"Well, 'Cumbaya,' of course," Stantz said. "But it also likes 'Everything Is Beautiful,' 'It's a Small World.' And anything by Jackie Wilson."

Stantz pushed a button on the cassette player and when "Higher and Higher" began blasting out, the slime began bubbling and cooing and even rocking with the music. But more amazing still was the fact that the toaster began doing it too! It was from the slime that had dripped into it.

Venkman couldn't believe what he was seeing. "This will be bigger than the Pet Rock!"

"Right," Spengler said. "And the first time someone gets mad, their toaster will eat their hand."

Venkman cocked his head and thought about it. "We'll put a warning on the label!" he suggested.

Later that evening Venkman was at home alone. There was a knock at his door. When he opened it he was surprised to see Dana and Oscar. Dana was wearing her nightgown and slippers with a coat and Oscar was wearing only a towel.

"Are we having a pajama party?" Venkman asked, letting them inside.

As far as Dana was concerned, it was no time for jokes. "Peter," she said, nearly frantic. "The bathtub tried to eat Oscar!"

She told him that she'd been bathing him when she'd noticed that instead of water, the tub was full of slime— and the slime tried to grab Oscar from her hands! She hadn't wasted time getting dressed.

"I must be losing my mind," Dana said. "At the museum today I could have sworn that terrible painting of Vigo looked right at me."

"Who could blame him?" Peter asked. "Were you wearing this nightgown?"

Peter was joking, but he had the feeling something was up—and that something was evil.

Peter helped Dana put some clothes on Oscar. He

loaned him his favorite sweatshirt. Then he called Stantz at the firehouse and told him to check out the situation at Dana's. Finally he invited Dana and Oscar to stay at his place. Dana agreed. Somehow, in spite of all his jokes and wisecracks, just being with Peter made her feel safe.

10

The next day Venkman met his friends outside the museum. Dana was still at his apartment. He didn't want her to leave until he was sure her own apartment was completely safe.

"Did you find anything at Dana's?" he asked when Stantz, Spengler, and Winston arrived.

"Nothing," Stantz said. "Just some mood slime residue in the bathtub. But we've been doing some research on Vigo the Carpathian. He was some bad dude! He was also known as Vigo the Cruel, Vigo the Torturer, Vigo the Despised—and those were the *nice* names! He dabbled in all the black arts—sorcery, witchery, alchemy, voodoo. And listen to his last words;—'Death is but a door, time is but a window. I'll be back.' "

Peter didn't like the sound of it. "Let's go give this guy another look," Venkman said. The Ghostbusters entered the museum and followed Venkman to the restoration studio.

Janosz tried to stop them, but he was helpless against the Ghostbusters.

"Let's sweep it, boys!" Stantz said to Spengler and Winston.

"That's the one that looked at Dana," Venkman told them, pointing to the portrait of Vigo. Janosz seemed more than a little nervous, but the painting didn't even wink.

"This entire room is extremely hot," Spengler said, consulting his P.K.E. meter. He gave the Giga-meter to Stantz. Stantz took samples from all around the room, and when he got to the portrait of Vigo, the indicator needle went off the top of the gauge. Stantz stared at the portrait. Unmoving, the portrait stared back at Stantz. Stantz seemed to feel the whole world fading. He was alone on earth with Vigo. Nothing else mattered—except Vigo. Lord, master, Vigo.

"Hey, that's some ugly dude!" Winston announced, coming up behind Stantz.

"Huh! what?" Stantz said, startled back to reality.

"You all right?" Winston asked.

"I'm fine," Stantz assured him. "I just got light-headed for a second there. We've got our readings now. Let's go." The rest of the Ghostbusters followed him out of the studio, through the hallways, out of the museum, and into Ecto-IA.

"There's definitely something going on," Spengler announced as Stantz pulled away from the curb. "The P.K.E. and giga levels were max-plus."

"I'd put my money on the Vigo character."

Nobody could disagree with that.

Suddenly the car swerved wildly. Stantz began honking and driving like a maniac. This wasn't like Stantz at all. He liked to use the siren, not drive over other cars!

"Going a little fast, aren't we, Ray?" Winston asked politely.

"Are you telling me how to drive?" Stantz snapped back. That wasn't like Stantz either. The Ghostbusters began to wonder if something had happened to him. When they looked at him and saw the vacant look in his eyes and the cruel sneer on his face, they *knew* something had happened—and that something had to be Vigo the Carpathian!

Ecto-IA continued to blast its way along the crowded street with Stantz at the wheel. Winston, Peter, and Egon held on for their lives while Stantz swerved through traffic. Then Stantz drove completely off the street and they were headed straight for a tree!

"Are you crazy, man? You're going to kill somebody!" Winston shouted.

Stantz's eyes seemed to glow bright red. "No! I'm going to kill *everybody*!"

That was too much for Winston. He made a fist with his right hand and—BAM!—he cold-cocked Stantz. Winston grabbed the wheel and reached across the front of the van to slam a foot on the brake. The Ectomobile skidded and stopped inches from the tree that might have been their end.

Shaken but unhurt, the Ghostbusters stumbled out of the van. Stantz blinked in confusion and rubbed his eyes. "What happened?" he asked. He sounded just like his old self. The red was gone from his eyes.

"You just lost the contest for Safe Driver of the Month," Venkman said.

"It was the strangest thing," Stantz told his friends. "I knew what I was doing, but I couldn't stop. This really terrible feeling came over me and I just felt like driving into a tree!"

The Ghostbusters examined the van. It had a few scratches on the bumper, but it would run all right. They climbed back in. Winston drove the rest of the way back to the firehouse. This episode had given the Ghostbusters an idea of the strength of their foe. They were going to have to give it everything to beat Vigo, but one thing they knew for sure, they weren't going to let him get the best of one of them again. Ever.

11

$\mathcal{L}$ater that night it was time to close up shop at the firehouse. Janine put the plastic cover on her computer terminal and began turning out lights. She thought she was alone, but she heard distinct loud noises from upstairs. She decided to investigate. She crept up the back stairs and peered into the lab area.

There was Louis Tully. He was completely swathed in a Ghostbusters coverall that was much too big for him. He had a proton pack strapped to his back. He held the nozzle in his hand. Slimer, the Ghostbusters' resident spook, was lurking in a corner. Slimer was a light greenish color, and potato-shaped. He had short arms and a weird sense of humor. He'd made friends with the Ghostbusters and liked to joke around with them. He'd never joked around with Louis. Louis didn't think he was going to start now.

Slimer stuck his thumbs in his ears and waggled his hands. He was making fun of Louis.

"Okay, Stinky, this is it. Showdown time. You and me, pal—"

Then he spun suddenly to where Slimer had been and shot a stream of protons. But all he hit was the ceiling and wall near where Janine was hiding. The proton stream burned a deep gash in the wall. Slimer had completely disappeared. Louis thought maybe he'd gotten him. Then he heard Slimer blow a raspberry!

Janine poked her head up. Louis realized he might have hit her!

"Oh, no! I'm sorry," Louis said, embarrassed. "I didn't mean to do that. It was an accident. I was just practicing, see. I'm like the fifth Ghostbuster." He hiked up his utility belt and the pants as well so he wouldn't trip on the cuffs. He forgot all about Slimer then. It was more fun to talk to Janine than to Slimer.

"Why would you want to be a Ghostbuster if you're already an accountant?" Janine asked.

"Well, it's just if one of the guys calls in sick or gets hurt," Louis explained.

"Oh, I see. Well, one didn't call in sick, but he needs some help. Want to come along?" Janine asked.

"Oh, sure!" Louis said eagerly. "I always want to help!"

"You can help tonight. See, I'm baby-sitting for Oscar because Dr. Venkman and Ms. Barrett are going out to dinner. It'll be just you and me." She smiled.

"Alone?" Louis gulped. And then he nodded. That could be more fun than busting ghosts! And it would definitely be more fun than trying to bust Slimer.

* * *

Venkman was surprised when he opened the door of his apartment. There, standing in front of him, were his partners, Stantz and Spengler, and Winston. They were wearing hip waders, firemen's slickers, miners' helmets, and they were carrying loads of sensing devices and photographic equipment.

"Don't tell me, let me guess. You're going to All-You-Can-Eat-Barbecue Rib Night at the Sizzler."

"We're going down into the sewer system," Stantz told him. "We want to see if we can trace the source of the psycho-reactive slime flow. We thought you might want to come along."

"Oh, I wish I'd known! I'd love to come along, but I'm stuck with these darn dinner reservations at Armand's, so toodle-oo and have a wonderful time!"

"Okay, but you're missing all the fun," Stantz said—and he sounded as if he meant it.

On their way back down the hallway at Venkman's, the Ghostbusters ran into the arriving baby-sitters. Louis and Janine stared at them in wonder. The Ghostbusters didn't offer any explanation, so Venkman provided one.

"They were helping change the diaper. It was a pretty messy one."

On that note Venkman and Dana departed for their evening on the town. Louis and Janine were alone—with Oscar.

12

The Ghostbusters, minus Venkman, landed quietly on the passenger platform of the nearly abandoned Van Horne Station—nearly abandoned except for a river of slime that swirled along the tracks.

"Let's get a sounding on the depth of that flow," Stantz said. He took out a cord with depth markings, weighted at the end with a plumb bob, and tossed it into the ooze. It quickly dropped to the bottom.

"Six feet . . . seven . . . eight," Spengler read as the plumb bob sank.

"That's it. It's on the bottom," Stantz said when the line stopped moving through his hand.

"Nine . . . ten . . . eleven . . ."

"Is the line still sinking?" Winston asked.

"No, the slime is rising!" Spengler said. And it was. It

was rising up over the edge of the platform. It was rising up over their boots!

"Let's get out of here, boys!" Stantz cried in alarm. He yanked to pull in the plumb line, but it was stuck. He called for help.

Winston and Spengler helped him pull the line, but it was no use. Not only that, but it was pulling them toward the depths of slime, and there was no stopping it.

Stantz tried to loosen his belt because the plumb line was attached to it, but his fingers fumbled and he couldn't get it off. While his friends watched in horror, Ray Stantz was pulled right into the malicious river of slime!

Spengler and Winston looked at one another. They couldn't let it happen to Ray. They had to do something! They jumped in after him. Within seconds all three Ghostbusters had been pulled down, down by the treacherous undertow of slime!

On the other side of town Venkman and Dana were enjoying their fancy dinner. Venkman poured the champagne. They toasted one another.

"So, are you making any New Year's resolutions?" Venkman asked. New Year's Eve was just one day away.

"I want to stop getting involved with men who aren't good for me," she said earnestly.

"Does that start exactly at midnight tomorrow or could you hold off for a few days, maybe?" Venkman asked hopefully.

Dana thought she'd have to think about that for a while. She wasn't really sure whether Venkman was no good for her—or whether he was the best thing that ever happened to her.

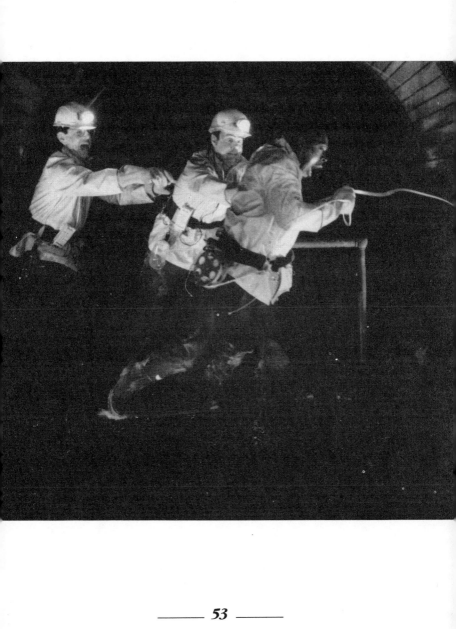

* * *

Meanwhile, back at the slime . . .

At the far end of the old abandoned railroad, where the slime pooled in the turnaround, a hand emerged from the mass. It grabbed at the ledge. It held tight. Another hand joined it. The rest of a body followed. It was Winston. He pulled himself up onto the safety of the platform and then bravely reached back into the slimy morass and took hold of a rubber-covered body that turned out to be Stantz. When Stantz was safe and had caught his breath, the two of them worked together and fished Spengler out of the gooey ooze.

Exhausted, the three slime-covered Ghostbusters looked for an escape from the tide of slime. There was a manhole cover above them—and a fragile, rusted iron ladder that reached it. One by one, the men climbed the ladder. One by one, they reached the relative safety of the streets of New York. One by one, they collapsed on the sidewalk, slime dripping from their slickers, their boots, their faces. . . .

They all felt nasty and mean. It seemed as if there were nothing rude and awful enough for them to say to one another.

"Nice going, Ray!" Winston sneered. "What were you trying to do? Drown me?"

"Look, Zeddemore," Stantz retorted. "It wasn't my fault you were too stupid to stay out of the slime!" He stood up and threatened to punch Winston.

Spengler jumped in. "If you two are looking for a fight, you got one. Who wants it first?" He asked menacingly.

"Butt out, pencil-neck!" Stantz snapped at Spengler.

"Strip! Right now!" Spengler cried. Following his lead, Stantz and Winston removed their slickers and

waders and then all the rest of their clothes—down to the long johns they were all wearing. Then they started to feel nice and normal again.

"What are we doing?" Winston asked. "Ray, I was ready to kill you." He slung a friendly arm across Ray's shoulders.

"It's the slime!" Stantz said, understanding clearly. "That stuff is like pure, concentrated evil!"

"And it's all flowing right to this spot!" Spengler said, pointing to where they stood, on the sidewalk, directly in front of the museum—where the painting of Vigo was being restored!

There wasn't a minute to waste!

13

Still just wearing their long johns, Winston, Spengler, and Stantz barged into Armand's. When they spotted Venkman and Dana they wove through the crowd of tables and began talking excitedly.

"You should have been there! Absolutely incredible!" Stantz began.

"Yeah, sorry I missed it," Venkman said, pouring another glass of champagne for Dana. "I guess you guys didn't know about the dress code here. It's really kind of a coat-and-tie place."

The threesome was still too excited about their discovery to think about little things—like clothes.

"It's all over the city, Pete—well, under it, actually," Stantz said.

"Rivers of the stuff!" said Winston.

"And it's all flowing toward the museum!" Spengler

finished. Venkman could see the implications of that clearly, but before they could act, Armand, himself, arrived at the table, along with two policemen.

"Arrest these men!" Armand said, pointing to the three men in their underwear.

"Hey! It's the Ghostbusters!" the policeman said. He was impressed. "But you're out of uniform, gentlemen," he said politely.

Stantz looked down and finally realized what he actually was wearing. He tried to cover himself with a menu.

"Uh, well, uh, we had a little accident," he stammered. "But forget that. We have to see the mayor as soon as possible."

The policeman looked at the trio doubtfully. It was hard to believe somebody standing in the middle of a fancy restaurant wearing long johns. "The mayor, huh? Well, they got a dinner party at Gracie Mansion tonight. You wouldn't want to interrupt that. Why don't you go home and get a good night's sleep and call His Honor in the morning?"

"We're not drunk and we're not crazy," Stantz informed the policeman. "This is a matter of vital importance!"

It took more arguing, but finally the policeman agreed to take the Ghostbusters, including Venkman, over to the mayor's house. Dana went back to Venkman's.

Dana found that things were very quiet back at Venkman's. Louis and Janine were sitting on the sofa very close to one another and Oscar was sound asleep. For some reason Dana felt relief. She made sure Oscar was covered snugly and then changed out of her evening dress. She wanted to be more comfortable to enjoy the rest of her quiet evening. Louis and Janine had offered to stay and keep her company until Peter got home. They were certainly quiet.

But just a few blocks away things were not so quiet. In the museum, above the ever-growing pool of bubbling slime, Vigo emerged from his portrait in all of his fierce red-and-black horror and hatred.

Janosz fell to his knees in front of his master.

"On a mountain of skulls in a castle of pain I sat upon a throne of blood. The rivers ran with tears! By the power of the Book of Gombotz I have waited for the time when the tide of men's sins would swell to bring me forth again. *Now* is that time and *here* is the place! The season of evil begins with the birth of the new year. Bring me the child that I might live again!"

"Yes, Lord Vigo," Janosz said, but then he had an idea. "Say, Lord Vigo, if I bring you the child, can I have his mother?"

"So be it!"

Vigo had commanded.

14

Ecto-IA followed the police car through the gates and into the driveway at the mayor's mansion. It pulled up in front of the door. The Ghostbusters got out. Stantz, Spengler, and Winston were now wearing police raincoats over their long johns. It wasn't exactly high fashion, but it *was* modest.

They waited in the mayor's private study, but they didn't wait long. His Honor and his aide, Hardemeyer, entered the study and closed the door. The mayor looked at his "guests" with disdain.

"All right. You've got two minutes. Make it good."

Stantz began. "Mr. Mayor, there is a psychomagnetheric slime flow of immense proportions building up under the city."

"Psycho-what?" the mayor asked.

Spengler continued. "We believe that negative human emotions are materializing in the form of a viscous, semiliquid, living, psycho-reactive plasma with explosive supranormal potential."

The mayor grimaced. "Does anybody here speak English?"

"Yeah, man," Winston said. "What we're trying to tell you is that all the bad feelings, all the hate and anger and violence of the city, are turning into this sludge. I didn't believe it at first, either, but we just took a bath in it and ended up almost killing each other."

"This is insane!" Hardemeyer interrupted. "Do we really have to listen to this?"

That was more than Venkman could take. "Hey, butt out!" he suggested. Then he turned to the mayor. "Look, Lenny, you have to admit there's no shortage of bad vibes in this town. There must be at least a couple of million miserable turkeys in the area. Here's a good example of one," he said, pointing to Hardemeyer.

Stantz took over. "This negative energy is building up—and if we don't do something, this whole place will blow—like a tomato on a hot plate!"

The mayor shook his head. They hadn't convinced him at all. "Being miserable and treating other people badly is every New Yorker's right, so none of this makes any sense to me, and if anything does happen, we've got plenty of paid professionals to deal with it. Your two minutes are up. Good night, gentlemen."

With that he turned and left the room. Hardemeyer, however, stayed. "That's quite a story," he said, smirking. "Would you consider telling this slime thing to some people downtown?"

Those were the words they *thought* they'd been waiting to hear. However, within a very short time they found themselves in a comfortably padded room talking to a psychiatrist who didn't believe a word they said but who took endless notes.

Hardemeyer was having them committed because he thought they were crazy.

Back uptown at Venkman's apartment, the power of Vigo was working its evil!

When Dana went into the bedroom to check on Oscar, she saw that his blankets were all pushed aside. Oscar was gone. And the window was open!

"Louis!" she yowled, and rushed to the window where Louis and Janine joined her.

There Dana saw her baby. He stood on the ledge at the corner of the building, fifty feet above the street. He was staring off into the distance—as if he were waiting for something.

Dana climbed out onto the ledge to save Oscar, but she was stopped cold by an apparition. It was a sweet and kind English nanny with the face of Janosz. The nanny reached out for Oscar. Oscar gurgled and took the nanny's hand. The nanny lifted Oscar and put him into a baby carriage—just like the one that had been commandeered by the slime—and took him away!

Dana watched the empty sky for a moment and then climbed back into the bedroom. "Louis," Dana said, "you have to find Peter and tell him what happened."

Louis was proud to be asked to help. It made him feel like a real Ghostbuster! He reached for his jacket and saw that Dana was doing the same. "Where are *you* going?" he asked.

"To get my baby back!" Dana said with determination.

15

Dana ran through the darkened museum. She knew who the enemy was—she knew where she had to go. She threw open the door to the restoration studio.

There, lying on the large table in the center of the room, was Oscar. He was sleeping contentedly. Dana rushed to pick him up.

"I knew you would come." It was Janosz. His voice oozed with sickly sweetness. He stood next to the painting of Vigo. "Don't worry. No harm will come to the child. He's been privileged, you see. And you too. You will be the mother of the ruler of the world. Doesn't that sound nice?"

"If you're any indication of what the world will be like, I don't want to live in it. I may not be able to stop you, but somebody will!"

"Who? The Ghostbusters? They are powerless. At midnight, just twenty-four hours away, with the coming of the New Year, the city will be mine—and Vigo's. So you see? You must marry me!" Janosz looked at Dana triumphantly. She didn't like the sound of any of this at all.

"I could never forgive what you've done to me and my child. I hate and despise you and everything you stand for with all my heart and soul."

Janosz shrugged off her cruel words. "Many marriages begin with a certain amount of distance, but after a while I believe we could learn to love each other. Think about it."

"I'd rather not," Dana told him.

She turned and picked up Oscar. He still slept as she headed for the door. But before she could leave the room Vigo sparked to life and reached out of the canvas, tossing bolts of restraining energy around Dana and Oscar. She couldn't move. She couldn't do anything to help herself . . . or her baby!

They were Vigo's prisoners!

16

The next morning, New Year's Eve, began as a bright sunny day, but it didn't stay that way for long because strange things started happening early in the day.

True to his word to Dana, Louis had found Peter, but it hadn't done anybody much good since Peter and the other Ghostbusters were locked up tighter than a drum in a psychiatric hospital. Even a writ of *habeas corpus* wouldn't get them out. So Louis tried the next best thing—bribery.

"Come on, Sherm, you're my cousin, remember?" Louis asked. "Do this for me, I'm begging you."

"Louis, I'm a skin doctor. I can't write orders for the psychiatric ward."

"I'll do your taxes for free. . . ."

"You *always* do my taxes for free and I remove your moles for free, remember?"

"Yeah, okay, then I'll get you out of those bad tax shelters."

"Of course you will. You got me into them!"

"I'll fix you up with Diane Troxler!"

"You already did. And I ended up removing *her* moles for free too. The answer is no!"

"Look, Sherm, I'm telling you. If we don't get those guys out, *now,* some weird and bad stuff is going to happen!"

Sherm looked at Louis dubiously, but he did notice, right then, that the sky seemed to be getting darker. It was only ten in the morning, and there were no clouds at all.

"Really weird stuff, I mean," Louis said.

As if on signal from Louis, really weird stuff started happening all over the city.

Slime began dripping from drainpipes and oozing up out of the gutters.

The Pulitzer Fountain, in front of the Plaza Hotel, began spouting psycho-reactive sludge.

A woman called the police to report dead people in the cemetery—walking around.

People at the natural history museum watched the brontosaurus stomp on the triceratops. The tyrannosaurus rex just laughed.

And then the *Titanic,* a luxury steamship that had sunk in the North Atlantic nearly eighty years ago, sailed into port!

And the sky got darker still.

"Good work, Louis," Stantz said as he and the other

Ghostbusters came out of the hospital. They were now wearing their proper uniforms, supplied by Louis. "How'd you get us out?"

"Oh, I pulled a few strings," Louis said casually. "I wouldn't want to say more than that—except that you've got to give Sherm a ride in Ecto-IA. Let him toot the siren, you know."

"Thanks, Louis. Thanks, Sherm," Stantz said. "We'll schedule that right after we rid the city of its current scourge. See you!"

With that the Ghostbusters piled into Ecto-IA, flipped on the flashing lights, sirens, and horns and left. There was work to do and they knew where they had to go to do it—the museum—temporary home of Vigo the Carpathian.

When they were within five blocks of the museum, their suspicions were confirmed. The streets were jammed with emergency vehicles. Ecto-IA honked its way through to the front. There, in all its glory, was the Manhattan Museum of Art, completely, totally, head to toe, covered with slime. In some places the slime was ten feet thick!

"It looks like a giant Jell-O mold," Stantz remarked, tightening the straps on his proton pack.

"I hate Jell-O," Venkman said thoughtfully.

The four men approached the fatigued fire fighters, who were attacking the slime with hacksaws, chain saws, and even the fabled Jaws of Life. But nothing worked.

"Give it a rest, Captain," Stantz said. "We'll take it from here."

"Full neutronas, maser assist," Spengler announced. The Ghostbusters adjusted their dials.

"Throw 'em!" Stantz commanded.

Bolts of proton energy spewed forth onto the doors of the museum, but it didn't make a dent in the hardened slime.

Venkman turned to the firemen. "Okay, who knows 'Cumbaya'?" he asked. Before they knew what was happening, all the firemen and the Ghostbusters and some bystanders found themselves holding hands, rocking gently back and forth, and singing, "Cumbaya, my Lord, cumbaya! Oh, Lord! Cumbaya!"

Nothing.

"Forget it," Stantz said. "The Vienna Boys Choir couldn't get through this stuff. I can't believe things have gotten so bad in this city that there's no way back. Sure, it's crowded, dirty, and noisy. And there are too many people who'd just as soon step on you as look at you. But there have got to be a few sparks of sweet humanity left in this burned-out city. We just have to mobilize it!"

Spengler nodded in agreement. "We need something that everyone can get behind. You know, a symbol!"

"Something that appeals to the best in each and every one of us!" Stantz added.

"Something good . . ."

"And pure . . ."

"And decent!" Winston concluded.

Then there was a commotion in the crowd. The mayor arrived, and hot on his heels was his hardheaded aide, Jack Hardemeyer.

Hardemeyer was really angry when he spotted the Ghostbusters. "I've had it with you! Get your stuff together, get back in that clown car, and get out of here. This is a city matter and everything's under control!"

"Oh, you think so?" Venkman asked coolly. "You've got Dracula's brother-in-law in there and he's got my

girlfriend and her baby. Around about midnight tonight, when you're partying uptown, this guy's going to come to life and start doing amateur head transplants—and that's just round one!"

"Are you telling me that there are people trapped in there?" the mayor asked. The Ghostbusters told him it was true. He turned to the fire captain. "Can you get into that museum?" he asked.

The captain shrugged. "If I had a nuclear warhead, then maybe."

The mayor turned to Venkman. "You know why all these things are happening?"

"Yes, sir."

"Can you do something about it?"

"Yes, sir," Venkman said.

This was more than Hardemeyer could stand. "Your Honor! You can't believe this mumbo jumbo! Can't you see? These guys put this stuff here! It's a big mess, but it's harmless. Just make them take it off!"

With that Hardemeyer pounded at the slime. He pounded so hard that his fist went right into the viscous mass—and the rest of his body was sucked in too. There wasn't a trace of him.

The mayor turned to the Ghostbusters. "Okay," he said grimly. "Just tell me what you need."

17

$\mathbb{I}$t was past sundown—or what *should* have been sundown. Because of the eclipse, the city had been dark since morning! The Ghostbusters were ready to begin their work in earnest. They had fewer than six hours to do the impossible, but it had to be done or the entire city would be enslaved by Vigo the Carpathian.

The special ferry dropped the Ghostbusters and Ecto-IA off on Liberty Island. They had brought all the equipment they thought they could possibly use. Each wore a specially made backpack consisting of tanks, hoses, and nozzles. The delicacy of the operation required careful monitoring, too, so each tank had lots of gauges and regulators.

"Kind of makes you wonder," Venkman said, gazing up at the mammoth Statue of Liberty.

"Wonder what?" Winston asked.

"Wonder what she's wearing under that toga!"

"There's nothing under that toga but three hundred tons of iron and steel," Spengler said.

"I hope we have enough stuff to do the job," Stantz said, echoing what everybody was thinking.

"Only one way to find out!" Venkman reminded them. They got to work.

First they lined the entire statue with wiring and speakers. That was the cake. Then it was time for the frosting. They sprayed every inch of the interior of the Statue of Liberty with psycho-reactive slime.

Meanwhile, back at the restoration studio . . .

Oscar was suspended in midair in front of Janosz. The painting of Vigo was dripping with fresh paint that Janosz put on his brush and used to paint strange markings on Oscar—the same strange markings and symbols that appeared in the background of Vigo's painting. Oscar cooed and giggled as the paint was smeared on his little chest and arms. Dana shivered with anger and fear, completely trapped by the evil of Vigo and his earthly enforcer, Janosz!

Meanwhile, back at the Ghostbusters' firehouse . . .

"Are you sure you know what you're doing?" Janine asked Louis. He was struggling to get into a Ghostbusters coverall. She helped him with the snaps. "Do the guys know you're doing this?"

"Oh, yeah, sure—no," he confessed, slipping his arms through the straps of the proton pack. "But there's really not much to do here and they might need some backup at the museum."

She secured the buckle on Louis's utility belt. "You're very brave, Louis," she said, smiling meaningfully. "Good luck." She kissed him.

Louis practically flew out of the firehouse to the street corner where he had to wait for a bus. After all, the other guys had Ecto-IA.

Meanwhile, back at the Statue of Liberty . . .

Stantz looked carefully at the work they'd done. "Seems okay to me," he said. "It's all yours now, Pete, but there isn't much time left!" He looked at his watch. It was 10 P.M. they had two hours to tame the slime!

"Okay," Venkman said, taking the challenge. "And a one—two—three—four!" He pushed the button on his portable cassette player and out it came—"Higher and Higher" by Jackie Wilson.

The Ghostbusters sang along too.

18

The Ghostbusters gathered in the observation deck in the crown of the Statue of Liberty and looked out the windows onto the New York harbor. They waited, listening to the music and singing along with it. Then, suddenly, they got what they'd been waiting for.

Stantz heard the rumble, then they all felt the motion. "She's moving!" Stantz cried victoriously.

"I've lived in New York all my life," Winston said. "And I never visited the Statue of Liberty. Now, I finally get here—and we're taking her out for a walk!"

"We've got full power!" Spengler announced, checking his Giga-meter.

"Okay, Libby, let's get it in gear!" Peter urged her.

There were more vibrations, then the statue lifted its right foot and stepped down from its pedestal. Splash! They were in the river, up to Liberty's hips!

"How deep does it go?" Winston asked. "I can't swim."

"Don't worry. I have my senior lifesaving card," Venkman said.

As it turned out, Liberty gave them a nice smooth ride to Manhattan. The water never got over her waist. Then she began the long trip uptown to the museum.

It was New Year's Eve. Everywhere throughout the city people were gathered waiting for the midnight celebration, fireworks, dancing, singing. As the Statue of Liberty and its four occupants strode uptown, partygoers cheered and waved. It was just what the Ghostbusters were hoping for. All that happiness and cheer was *just* what the slime needed—maybe even more than "Higher and Higher."

By eleven-thirty they'd reached Times Square—heart of the world's New Year's Eve celebration. The whole place was jammed with revelers waiting for the brightly lit ball to descend and bring on the new year. Then, with a few loud thumps, Liberty approached the mass of people. The crowd heard the familiar strains of "Higher and Higher" and began dancing with joy.

Spengler checked the Giga-meter. "It's working!" he cried. "The positive G.E.V.'s are climbing like crazy."

Venkman patted the interior of the statue. "They love you, Lib," he said reassuringly. "Keep it up."

The cheers of the crowd sent them on uptown, through the theater district, across the southern end of Central Park. The museum was in sight.

"So far, so good," Venkman said, his confidence building.

"I'm worried," Spengler told him. "The vibrations

could shake her to pieces. We should have padded her feet."

"I don't think they make Reeboks her size," Stantz observed. "And we don't have time to stop at Shoe-Town. It's almost midnight!"

"We're almost there, Lib. Step on it!"

And she did. She stepped right on a car and squished it flat as a pancake.

Stantz stuck his head out a window of the observation deck. "My fault!" he called out to the flat car.

"She's new in town!" Venkman yelled in explanation.

Back in Times Square, the excitement built up in the crowd. It was just sixty seconds until the new year!

"In sixty seconds my life begins!" Vigo uttered from the prison of his canvas. "Then woe to the weak. All power to me!"

Janosz continued painting symbols on Oscar's body. He was working frantically. He had to finish by midnight!

The crowd in Times Square began the fifteen-second countdown. "Fifteen . . . fourteen . . . thirteen . . ."

"Come on, Lib! Just a few more giant steps!" Venkman said. He could see the museum. He knew Dana and Oscar were inside and they needed his help!

"Nine . . . eight . . . seven . . ."

Just one more symbol to go—a quick and easy one. Janosz put fresh paint on the brush and began the final symbol. Vigo's eyes glowed with joy. Janosz worked by the light of the bright New Year's moon, which glowed through the skylight in the studio. But suddenly the light disappeared. It was completely shadowed by something very big. Janosz looked up and found himself staring into the angry face of the Statue of Liberty. Before he could gasp the statue smashed the skylight windows with her torch and the Ghostbusters came sliding into the studio on ropes.

"Happy New Year!" Venkman said to Janosz. But he was too early. It wasn't midnight yet. The Ghostbusters had won the race—now all they had to do was win the battle!

19

$\mathcal{D}$ana grabbed Oscar from Janosz, who was too surprised, and too angry, to object. She fled with her baby, taking him to safety, out of Janosz's reach.

From his canvas prison Vigo began yowling in fury. Janosz stepped in front of the painting.

"Hi, there," Venkman greeted him while aiming his proton nozzle. "Feel free to try something stupid."

Janosz wasn't ready to admit defeat. "You pitiful, miserable creatures! You dare to challenge the power of darkness? Don't you realize what you are dealing with? He's Vigo! You are like the buzzing of flies to him!"

Venkman shook his head sadly and sighed. "Oh, Johnny. You really backed the wrong horse this time."

With that the Ghostbusters blasted Janosz, covering him in sweet, loving slime from head to toe. A kind smile came across his face. He began humming "Higher and Higher."

Then the Ghostbusters turned to Vigo. He had pulled himself free of the canvas from his knees up, but his legs were still firmly held, and his ultimate power had been neutralized by the loving warmth of the goodwill of the citizens of New York and their kindly ambassador of love and international friendship, the Statue of Liberty.

Vigo snarled at the Ghostbusters, snatching weakly at their backpacks. His magic wasn't working, and his wrath was nothing but watered-down anger.

The Ghostbusters squared off against their enemy. Venkman taunted and teased him. "There, there, now, Vigo," he said. "You have been a naughty little monkey and you're going to have to be punished."

"The whole city's together on this one," Stantz told the Carpathian. "We took a vote. The mayor got reelected. You didn't."

"Say good night now!" Winston said sweetly.

They adjusted their gauges to blast their nemesis, but Vigo wasn't ready to give up. Before the stream of loving kindness hit him, he stepped out of the canvas, grabbed Stantz, and held him tightly. As soon as Vigo touched him, Ray's eyes became glassy. He looked as if he were in a trance.

"Don't do it!" Spengler said, warning his buddies not to fire. "You'll hit Ray!"

"Command me, lord," Ray said to Vigo. He was becoming Vigo's slave, just the way Janosz had been. There wasn't a second to spare!

The instant the slime hit Vigo he released Stantz and then fell back onto the canvas. Stantz stumbled away and collapsed, gasping. Vigo turned from fearful monster to oozing liquid paint and melted completely off the canvas. He ended up in a totally harmless pool of goo.

When they were sure Vigo was gone for good, the Ghostbusters turned their attention to their friend Stantz.

Spengler examined him. He opened up his coverall to give him air. He checked his pulse and respiration. "He's breathing," Spengler announced.

Winston wiped the slime off Stantz's face. His eyes blinked open. "Ray, Ray. How do you feel, man?" Winston asked.

A happy and warm smile passed across Stantz's face. "Groovy! I've never felt better in my life!"

The Ghostbusters helped Ray to his feet. "I love you guys," Ray said. "You're the best friends a guy ever had."

"Oh no," Venkman groaned. "We've got to live with Mr. Sweetness and Light?"

Venkman might have gone on complaining except that Stantz hugged him. It made it hard to complain. Then he hugged Winston and Spengler, spreading the loving slime all over all of his friends.

Venkman, in turn, went to hug Dana, who was only too happy to hug him back. And then they *both* hugged Oscar.

"What's this? A love-in?" Venkman asked, a little embarrassed by all the affection he was showing. Nobody else seemed to mind. He picked up Oscar and began washing the weird signs and symbols off his little chest and arms. Oscar cooed and gurgled happily.

"I think he likes you," Dana said. "And I think I do too."

"Finally come to your senses, huh?" he asked.

She nodded and gave him a great big kiss.

On the other side of the room the Ghostbusters

helped Janosz to his feet. He'd been completely trans-
formed, back to just plain Janosz. He wasn't Vigo's slave
anymore. "What happened?" he asked, very confused.

"Sir, you had a violent, prolonged, transformative
psychic episode. but it's over now. Want some coffee?"

"That's very kind of you," Janosz said sweetly.

Spengler checked him from head to toe with every
instrument he was carrying. "Janosz is fine," he told his
friends. "Physically intact and psychomagnetherically
neutral."

Janosz looked at him in surprise. "Is that good?" he
asked.

"It's where you want to be," Winston said.

"Hey, let's go celebrate the New Year," Venkman said.
He could hear the crowd standing outside the museum
cheering. They all wanted to be part of the happiness.

They turned to leave, but on the way out they
noticed a real change in the painting that had once been
Vigo's portrait. Once the slimy paint that had portrayed
Vigo had been wiped off the canvas, they could see that
Vigo had actually been painted on *top* of another painting. This one portrayed four angels hovering over a little
baby. The funny part was that the baby looked a lot like
Oscar. And the four angels—well, one wore glasses, one
was a little stocky, one had curly dark hair and an
irrepressible grin. And the fourth looked a lot like Winston Zeddemore.

"There's something very familiar about this painting," Winston remarked.

"No way," Janosz assured him. "It's been covered by
Vigo for centuries!"

Winston shrugged and followed his friends out to
where the merrymakers were gathered in front of the
museum.

Should old acquaintance be forgot,
And never brought to mind?

It was past midnight and thousands of people were gathered in front of the museum singing "Auld Lang Syne" in celebration of the New Year and the Ghostbusters' conquest of the evil of Vigo. All the wicked slime that had covered the museum was completely gone. A new spirit of love filled everybody there. It was truly a kinder, gentler New York that greeted the Ghostbusters.

It was also Louis who greeted them. He stumbled off a crosstown bus, completely garbed in his Ghostbuster outfit. He waved good-bye to the driver of the bus. The driver was his new friend, Slimer.

Louis was glad that he and Slimer were friends. Friends did things together.

"Okay, so Monday night, we'll get something to eat and maybe go bowling? Can you bowl with those little arms?"

Slimer spurted a little friendly slime at Louis in farewell and then slammed the bus door shut.

Louis hurried up the museum steps.

"Am I too late?" he asked Stantz.

"No, you're right on time!" Stantz assured him. Stantz popped the cork off a bottle of champagne and handed it to Louis.

Just then Hardemeyer stumbled out of the museum. He, too, had been released from the prison of hatred and anger by the Ghostbusters.

"Happy New Year, everybody!" he cried, flinging a loving arm around Spengler's shoulders. Hardemeyer's eyes filled with tears of love and joy. He chimed in on the chorus of "Auld Lang Syne."

20

Never had the city been so filled with happiness! Everybody was living with the joy of love and warmth and kindness. Everybody, that is, except the mayor. He had a little problem on his hands.

The Ghostbusters met him out behind the museum later that night. They found the mayor standing next to the Statue of Liberty. She was lying flat on her back. She'd dropped her torch and looked like she was tired from all the walking.

"She's all right," Venkman told His Honor. "She's only taking a little nap."

"We just had it restored and now it's ruined! It'll cost us millions—maybe billions. Can you do something?"

The Ghostbusters exchanged glances. This *could* be the chance they'd been waiting for. Venkman spoke first.

"Uh, this probably isn't a good time to bring this up,

but the last time we did a job for the city, we never got paid."

The mayor looked at him in surprise.

"This is a bill for tonight's job," Stantz said, handing the stunned man a piece of paper. When he looked at it he was even more stunned.

"What! This is way too much! We won't pay."

Venkman looked at the Statue of Liberty sprawled out on the cold ground. "I think she looks pretty good here, don't you?" he asked Stantz.

"Yeah, and a lot more convenient than on that silly island. In the middle of the harbor. So far away."

The mayor's goose was cooked. "All right. All right. I'll get you a check on Monday."

"Sorry," Spengler said. "No checks. Cash only. Company policy."

The mayor glared at them, but he agreed.

Several weeks later the winter sun gleamed down on the freshly cleaned copper of the Statue of Liberty as she stood, guarding New York's harbor, in the same way she had for over a hundred years. Once again she was the city's symbol of love, peace, understanding, and goodness.

"Pretty impressive, huh?" Venkman asked, looking up at the statue.

"Yeah," Stantz agreed. "Just think, people have seen her here, exactly like this, for such a long time."

"Not *exactly* like this," Spengler said.

There was something about Spengler's tone of voice that made Venkman nervous.

"What do you mean?" Venkman asked cautiously.

"Well, for one thing, today she's got the torch in her

left hand and the book in her right hand. It *used* to be the other way around!"

Venkman looked back up at the statue and then he looked at his friends. He leaned forward and put his finger to his lips.

"Shhh," he said. "Nobody'll notice. But *if* they do, who are they going to call?"